Chai Aur Tum

Sukoon ka Dusra Naam

Flairs and Glairs

House

Disclaimer

This is a work of fiction and solely represent the thoughts of the corresponding authors of the articles. Our editors have tried their best to edit the content of all the authors and check the plagiarism.

All the write-ups in this book are unique and are only published in this book.

In case any plagiarism or error is found, only the author is responsible alone, and not the publisher or the Compilers.

Cover Designing and Book Formatting
Shubham Shah and Ishani Agarwal

Acknowledgment

Dear Almighty, thank you for blessing me with the power and zeal to be able to complete this Anthology.
Also, Thank You dear parents, for trusting in me, and letting me work whenever I wanted. My family is the one who supported me for what I am today.
When it comes to this, Anthology, I would like to start with Thanking the Co -Authors, without your help and support, I would have never been able to complete it.
Thank you all of you, for being there. Much Love to all of you. I am glad to see you all standing by me.

Co Author

Shubham Shah (Founder Flairs and Glairs)
Ishani Agarwal (Co-Founder Flairs and Glairs)
Shivangi Jaiswal (Compiler)

1. Mandavi Singh
2. Bhavika Dhiraj Sindhi
3. Isshu Sami
4. Saloni Lal Srivastava
5. Shivansh Sharma
6. Dr. Rakesh R Mund
7. Jaspreet Kaur
8. Kirti Goel
9. Ronak Jain
10. Kuldeep Sharma
11. अभय कुमार
12. Rohan "Vikramaditya"
13. Sheetal Ahuja
14. Mansvi Kathiriya
15. Sushmita Mishra
16. Maniska Das
17. Khushi Agrawal
18. Agrima Viraj
19. Rinitha Priya J
20. Ananya Mohanty
21. Ms. Ishrat Jahan Noormohammed Khan
22. Hitesha Sahani
23. Lingampally Pradeep Reddy
24. Mehak Bhan
25. Rudransh Bhattacharya
26. Sayandeep Patra
27. Vishal K R
28. Jayati Thakar

Shubham Shah

(Founder- Flairs and Glairs)

Shubham Shah, an entrepreneur at "Flairs & Glairs" a brand with dynamics in events organizing and cultural educational pan INDIA, is a 26yrs old guy who recently has entered the digital platform of imprinting emotions. He has initiated with his own open mic platform to help budding poets and aspiring writers under his brand named as "Teekhe Zasbaaat"

He is a commerce graduate from the Bhagalpur City of Bihar.
He states Writing has impersonated him since childhood and he has now been writing for over a decade!
Cooking, on the other hand, is his passion! He also mentions, trying out new things just tickles him!
When asked sir, Why SPICY EMOTIONS?
He smiled and added, "agar jasbaat teekhe na ho toh wo jasbaat kahan" Spices are all that blends! So do his words!
As a chef, he presents to you his dish! Hot and freshly served! Taste it! Feel it! Enjoy it! You can also find his writing in the Book "Teekhe Zasbaaat" and 50+ Co -authored anthologies. With his passion to explore opportunities across Platforms, he is working with keen dev otion and We wish him all the very best for his future ventures.
He is Featured in the International Magazine DeMode for his upcoming solo novel.
He is Approved by Ne8x for its Lit Fest, and is a Golden Star Awards 2020 Winner.
He is a India Book of Records Holder for his Anthology Satrang, and has the Grandmaster title by Asia Book of Records, for the same.
He has also been featured in Prabhat Khabar, Dainik Jagran, and a lot of other Newspapers in Bihar for his achievements.
He has been a proud co-author to
India Book Of Records (Title- Black)
World Book Of Records (Title -15 Wonders of Poetries)
India Book Of Records (Title - Aaina)
Vajra World Records Holder (Title - Gustakhi Maaf Hai)
High Range of Records Holder (Title - Gustakhi Maaf Hai)
Indian Book of Records
(Title - Road from Worst to Best)

Share your reviews on his

INSTAGRAM

       @spicy_emotions

       @shubham4shah

Or via email on

       shubham2shah@gmail.com

To stay tuned to his work and opportunities follow his business Handles

INSTAGRAM   FACEBOOK   YOUTUBE

       @flairsandglairs

       @teekhezasbaaat

WEBSITE:

       https://flairsandglairs.in/

       https://flairsandglairs.com/

Ishani Agarwal

(Co-Founder- Flairs and Glairs)

Ishani Agarwal hails from the City of Joy, Kolkata.
She is the co -founder of her Community "Teekhe Zasbaaat"
and Flairs and Glairs Publication.
Been a Compiler for 45+ Anthologies, she is in the process for
more. Co-authored in 150+ Anthologies. She is a India Book
of Records Holder, a Vajra World Records Holder, a High
Range of Records Holder, an OMG Book of Records Holder,
a Bravo Record holder, a Forever Star Book of World Records
and an Indian Book of Records Holder.
Approved by Ne8x for its Lit Fest 2020, and Literary Icon
2020. Also a Golden Star Awards Winner 2020.
She has also been award ed with India Star Republic Award
2021, a part of She Awards by Awards Arc and Winner of Nari
Samman 2021 by Literoma.

She is also selected as Best Achiever of the Year by AwardsArc and Most Challenging Compiler Award by Spectrum Awards.
She got her first solo Published,a solo Compilation consisting of first 750 contents of hers, titled "Hand That Burnt While Healing".

She has been featured by the National Magazine "Taree Zameen Par" with the title 'unstoppable'.
Also featured in the International Magazine DeMode for her upcoming solo novel, she is proud to write on social issues, and is happy with the love she is receiving.
Connect with her on Instagram: @Ishani_agarwal_quotes / @compilations_so_far

Shivangi Jaiswal
(Compiler)

Shivangi Jaiswal is a Content Writer from Kolkata. Executive Head at "Flairs & Glairs" brand with dynamics in events organizing and cultural educational pan INDIA. Organizer at "The Glittering Fables" Writing Community. She is a B. Com Honors graduate. Certified in Stocks & Short Selling as well as Certified in Digital Marketing Been a keen student, she has recently been Certified for learning Spanish Language.
She is an Indian Book of Record Holder.

Approved by Ne8x for its Lit Fest 2020 for the Author of the Year 2020 and the Real Hero's Title 2020. Also, a Warrior of Change Awardee 2021

She loves to bring smiles and happiness to many faces, so she is into Social service.

Traveler, Teacher, Meditator, Dancer, Singer, Instrument Player. She loves to play guitar and harmonium. Also been awarded in many events for winning many categories Been a Public Speaker she has taken part in many events and nailed it. Been a great Advisor to many. She has also been crowned for winning Miss Great Podium 2020 Title in the category Modelling recently. Sports freak of Swimming and Badminton with a passion so strong. Since, past one year she has started her writing journey.

She writes so that many people can connect with their stories and get positive hopes. She thinks " Every story is unique so embrace yourself to the best". She is a writ   er by day and a reader by night. Been a Complier of 3 2+ Anthologies, and in process for more, also Co - authored 1 20+ anthologies. Shivangi is an old soul with young eyes, a vintage heart, and a beautiful mind."

You can follow her work:
Instagram
@the_knockingvibe
@house_of_compilations

Beautiful Aroma That Touched My Heart.

Spilling tea from the cup.
Or maybe happiness was spilling from your deep eyes.

The beautiful aroma touching my heart
And making me skip a beat.

Seems like you were adding sweetness in my heart with
wonderful touching flavor.
But the sweetness was lesser than your precious smile.

Which was making my heart beat faster.
Tea with beautiful smile served
The beautiful aroma with a magical sparkle in your eyes.

A kind of spark was lighting between us.
Neither I nor you had tea,
But our eyes meet and lips kissed.

Looking into each other's deeply lost.
Destination met over a cup of tea.

Sukoon Ka Phela Naam Ho Tum

Sukoon ka phela naam ho tum
Meri bandagi meri Aashiqui ho tum.

Voh subah subah tumhara yu mujhe jagana
Meri hoothon ko chu kar meri subah khushnuma banana.

Tumhare pyar se ghula voh ek ek chuski
Elaichi si sugandh, Adrak si tazgi.

Savala sa rang tumhara,
Thoda karak mijaj hai.
Mohobbat ki kami ko puri karni ki chah ho tum,
Sach kahu toh Do dilo ko milane ki chaahat ho tum.

Ab zindagi ki har khubsurat chiz aur behtar ho jati hai
tumhare sath.
Voh pal sach main bahut khaas hai,
Thakan se rahaat aur hothon par bas tumhara naam hai.

Chalo ek sawal karu…
Tumhara aur Chai ka kya rishta hai?

Tu na mile toh kuch khali khali sa lagta hai.
Tere bina main jeena sochu bhi kaise.
Kyuki, Bas teri ek Jhalak aur tazgi hi mere zindagi ki jeet hai.

Mandavi Singh

Mandavi singh is a native of Kanpur U.P. She has completed her PGDBA in HR and currently working as a HR with Digi Grow Hub. she loves to explain herself through beautiful words. she writes poetry story and also lyrics.
Follow her for more write ups: Instagram - @singh_mandavi_

चाई की टापरी

तुमको देखा तो ये खयाल आया
जिन्दगी धूप तुम घना साया-२
आज फिर दिल ने एक तमन्ना की-२
आज फिर दिल को हमने समझाया
जिन्दगी धूप..

बारिश कीं बूंदों में लिपटे ठण्ढे हवा के झोकें हाथ मे गरम चाय का कप और सोंधी खुशबू मे घुली जगजीत जी की ग़ज़ल जिन्दगी का ये पल तब तक तो बडा सुकून भरा था जब तक टपरी मे निशांत नहीं आया था।

निशांत मेरा सहपाठीऔर जबरन अपने आपको को मेरा दोस्त कहने वाला मेरा मूहँ बोला मित्र निशांत से मेरी मुलाकात कॉलेज e के पहले दिन ही हो गई थीं पर बातचीत करीब एक महीने बाद चाय कीं टपरी में हुई जब महाराज अपने तीसरे संबंध विच्छेद
का शोक मनाने मेरे पास आ कर बैठ गये। उसके एक भी सवाल का ठीक से जवाब ना देने के बावजूद उसने अपनी तीनों प्रेम कहानियों का शुरुआत औ अंत बता डाला। मेरी चाय खत्म होते ही मैंने   चाय   के   पैसे   दिए   और औपचारिकता के लिए बोला ""सुन के बुरा लगा"" और ""   बाय"" कह कर जाने लगी। मेरे byee कहते ही वें बोला
अरे..।।
""जा रही हो पर तुमने अपना नाम तो बताया हीं नहीं""
मेरे ""निशा"" बोलते ही जनाब के चेहरे से तीनों breakup का दर्द ऐसे छू हुआ जैसे कभी कुछ हुआ हीं नहीं था। फिर वे थोड़ा टेढा मुस्कुराया और बोला ""वैसे हमारी दोस्ती बुरी नहीं होगी तुम निशा मैं निशांत,सही है ना"" तब से महाराज जबर्दस्ती मेरे दोस्त हुए पडे है।
मैं एक बार प्यार मे बुरी तरह हार चुकी थीं जिसका गहरा असर हुआ था मेरे दिल और दिमाग में मैंने दोस्ती को काम पडने पर निभाया जाने वाला एक मतलबी रिश्ता बना के रख दिया था। दिल से दोस्ती

करना छोड़ दिया था मैंने। ना जाने कितने दिनों बाद कोई बडे हक से मेरे जिन्दगी में आ गया था।उस दिन के बाद निशांत कॉलेज मे ज्यादातर मेरे साथ ही रहता था। फिर कभी मैं चाय कीं टपरी में अकेले नहीं जा पाई ,साये सा साथ रहने लगा था वे मेरे कभी कुछ भी काम हो निशांत बिना कहें ही मेरे पास होता। थोड़ा ज्यादा बकवास करता था पर ना जाने क्यों उसका साथ उसकी बक-बक कीं आदत सी पड गई थीं।जिस दिन वो कॉलेज

मे ना होता वहाँ मेरा मन नहीं लगता उसके बिना पी गई चाय अब फीकी सी लगाने लगीं थी।उसके साथ college के लगभग दो साल कैसे बीत गये मालूम ही नहीं चला।इन दो सालों मे निशांत मुझे दो बार प्रस्ताव

कर चुका था पर मैं कभी उसे हाँ नहीं कर पाई ऐसा नहीं था कि मै उसपर विश्वास नहीं करती थी । उसपर तो मैं खुद से ज्यादा विश्वास करने लगीं थी ।पर उसके प्रस्ताव

को कभी accept नहीं कर पाई ।शायद उसे खोने से डरती थी।दो साल पहले खुद से भागते हुए मम्मी पापा के फैसले के खिलाफ मैं MBA करने के बहाने यहाँ बैंगलोर आई थी।सोचा था अब इस जिन्दगी में फिर किसी को हिस्सा नहीं दूंगी । मेरे लाख ना चाहने पर भी निशांत इसका एक अहम किरदार बन चुका था।

पर कल जो हुआ उसके बाद शायद अब निशांत कभी लैट कर नहीं आयेगा।वो कितने प्यार से पहली बार मेरे धर आया था सिनेमा की टिकटेंले कर औऱ मैंने कितनी बेरुखी से ना सिर्फ टिकटें फाढ़ दिया बल्कि कितना भला बुरा भी कहा उसे बस इसी डर से की कहीं वो फिर मुझे प्रस्ताव

ना कर दें औऱ अब मुझमें इतनी ताकत नहीं बची थी की उसे फिर मना कर सकूं।

मैं हमेशा उसे थोड़ा कम बोलने को कहती थी पर आज जब वो मेरे सामने से बिना कुछ कहें चुपचाप चला गया है तो उसकी वो खामोशी मुझे अन्दर ही अन्दर खाये जा रहीं हैं।

यूँ तो निशांत कल शाम को ही यहाँ से चला गया था पर ना जाने क्यों अब भी उसे अपने बहुत करीब महसूस कर रही थी । चाय की टपरी मे हमारी पहली बातचीत से लेकर कल शाम को जो कुछ भी हुआ एक एक कर सब याद आ रहा था मुझे ।निशांत को याद करते हुए एक पूरी रात यही कुर्सी मे बैठे बैठे गेट को निहारते हुए निकल दी थीं मैंने कि शायद कोई आहट हो और निशांत वापस आ जाए कभी लौट के ना जाने के लिए । सुबह एक आहट पा के दौड़ कर गेट खोला तो वहाँ कोई नहीं था। मायूस हो कर लौटते कदम ना जाने क्यों जोर से सीड़ियों की तरफ जोर से भागे और देखा की निशांत सीड़ियों पर बैठा था । मैं चुपचाप उसके करीब जा कर बैठ गई थोड़ी देर बाद निशांत उठ कर जाने लगा। मैंने उसकी तरफ देखा तो उसके होठों पर मुस्कान थी आँखों में एक अलग सी चमक थीं।

जाने अनजाने मैंने उसका हाथ पकड़ लिया था ।उसके बढ़ते कदमों के साथ अब मेरे कदम भी बढ़ने लगें थें और हर बढते कदम के साथ मजबूत हों रही थी हमारे हाथों की पकड़ जैसे कभी अलग ना होने का वादा कर रही हो एक दूसरे से...

Bhavika Dhiraj Sindhi

Bhavika Dhiraj Sindhi a 25-year-old
creative writer. She belongs to Turkey an Indian writing from
abroad due to her passion in writing. a curious girlA wanderer
who likes to explore new things and places a hardheaded but
softhearted
She uses her pen as a best friend to speak her feelingsBelieves
only love can make this place a better to survive...!

मेरी ज़िन्दगी

कुछ लोगों ने मुझसे पूछा कि आपके लिए "सुकून" क्या है???

माँ ने आपनी गोद में मुझे सुलाया।

पापा न सर पर हाथ फेर दिया ।

दादाजी पार्क घूमने लेके चले!

दादीजी ने छुपकर पैसे दिए चॉकलेट लाने के लिए!

और बडा भाई टी. वी के रिमोट के लिए लड़ा। हमने कहाँ कि बस यही सुकून है,जो हमें जीवन में मिला|

ये तो वो बचपन के दिन थे जो भूले नहीं जाते।

वरना आज कल की दौड़ती ज़िंदगी में सुकून कहाँ।

इस बदलते वक़्त की रफ़्तार के साथ हम भी बड़े हो गए।

कॉलेज की डिग्री लेने गाँव से शहर आ गए इस अकेले शहर में चाय के अलावा हमारा कोई न था

कॉलेज के बाहर वही चाय की टपरी चाय पीते पीते तुम्हारी आँखों से एक मुलाक़ात हो गई उस रात हम चाय पीते रहे और वो आँखें हमें सोने नहीं दे रही थीं।

इस छोटे से दिल को वो आँखों की चमकती हुई रोशनी तो उसे प्यार कर रही थी।

क्लास का मोनिटर बन कर दोस्त बन गए थे ।

पहली बार लगा पढ़ाई कुछ काम आयी ।

तुमसे यूं रोज़ मिलना बातें करना बड़ा अच्छा लगता था ।

लेकिन तुम्हें कहने की हिम्मत नहीं हुई कि हमें तुमसे मोहब्बत है ।

ऐसा लगता है मानो तुम्हें पाना एक तारे को पाने जैसा था लेकिन एक डर भी था उसे टूटने का यानी तुम्हें खो देने का ।

देखते देखते तीन साल बीत गाए रोज़ शाम की तरह मैं चाय पी रहा था

इससे इत्तेफ़ाक़ कहूँ या भागवान का मेरी तम्मना पूरी करना ।

बारिश अचानक होने लगीं और तुम मेरे पास उस पेड़ के नीचे आ खड़ी हुई मैंने बस पूछ लिया चाय पियोगी इस बरसात में इसका अलग़ ही सुकून है ।जिस तरह तुम्हें देखकर मुझे मिलता है इस भीड़ मे..

ना जाने वो हिम्मत कहाँ से आई हम में कैसे आयी।

लगा सपने में हमने कहा ।

लेकिन तुम पास ही थीं।

वो तुम्हारा मुस्कुराना मानो १० सेकंड के लिये मेरी धड़कने थम गई।

वो पल आज भी मेरे दिल की धड़कने तेज़ कर देता है वो तुम्हारा मुस्कुराना और कहना ज़िंदगी भर का सुकून दे सकतीं हूँ ।

और आज भी हम रोज़ शाम ऑफिस के बाद उस चाय की टपरी पर मिलकर चाय पीते है।

वो चाय और तुम मेरी ज़िंदंगी के सुकून बन गए हो।

तो मेरे संतुलन जीवन का रहस्य है आप और यह चाय का प्याला।

इसलिए मैं चाहता हूँ कि इस एक कप चाय के साथ आप हमेशा के लिए साथ रहें!

Isshu Sami

Born and brought up in Nagpur, He loves to write and travel.
He is a dance and Drama choreographer but he wants to pursue
his career as writer in future!

(1)

Mujhe Ek buri Adat Hai.
Haa mujhe Ek buri Adat Hai .
Main Khushi mein, Gum mein, Tanhaiyo mein chai pita hu.
Jaise mano koi sharabi hu
Par sharab ki jagah chai pita hu.
Kabhi koi biscuit ko Qurbaan Kar deta hu chai ke pyale mein
Kabhi bhul ata hu pyala hi building ke aakhri male pein.
Chai aur Mera rishta kuch aasmaa or Badal sa hai
Log Aksar kehte hai mujhe "kitni chai pita hai!! Yeh ladka
pagal sa hai"
Or bohot zyada khush ho jau ya thakaan badan todne lage ..
Haal behaal sa ho bekhudi muh modne lage..
Toh chai ke sath ek sutta bhi laga leta hu.
Haa haa malum hai Fefdo ke liye sutta bada
Afaat hai!!
Par jaisa meine kaha ki
Haa mujhe Ek buri adat hai!!

Saloni Lal Srivastava

She is Saloni Lal Srivastava daughter of Mr. Kumar Prashant and Mrs. Asha Sinha from Siwan, Bihar. She is currently, working as a Project Coordinator under Flairs & Glairs Publication House.

And also, purchasing B.sc in Botany honors.

Her life is all around her family, friends and career.

She has also worked as coauthor in 30+ anthologies.

She is the one who loves to spread smile and positivity to everyone.

You can follow her on Instagram: @salonilalsrivastava.

(1)

डियर सुकून,

चाय और तुम क्या कहूं मैं अब इस बारे में। एक जमाना था जब चाय मुझे बिल्कुल भी पसंद नहीं थी और तुम्हे हद से ज्यादा। मैं कॉफी की दीवानी थी तो तुम चाय के। हम जब कभी मिलते तो हमारा झगड़ा बस एक ही बात पर होता चाय अच्छी है तो कॉफी अच्छी है और तुम हर बार मेरा दिल रखने के लिए कॉफी अच्छी है पर मान जाते। याद तुम्हे जब हम पहली बार मिले थे। तुमने अनजाने में दो कप चाय मंगा लिया था। तब मेरी शकल देखने लायक थी। फिर तुमने मेरा झललाया हुआ चेहरा देखकर। बड़ी ही मासूमियत से पूछा " ऐसा क्या हुआ जो तुम्हारा मासुम सा चेहरा उतर गया ? " फिर उतनी ही खामोशी भरा मेरा जवाब था " बस चाय पसंद नहीं " और मेरी मासुमियत देख तुम खिलखिला उठे। तुम्हे खिलखिलाता देख मेरी चिढ़ मानो जैसे और बढ़ गई। फिर हमारी हर मुलाकात पर तुम्हारा चाय ऑर्डर करना और मेरा चिढ़ाना। यह तो जैसे सिलसिला ही बन पड़ा। तब तुम मेरे सुकून थे और यह चाय बेसुकूनी। आज आलम यह है कि तुम तो ना जाने कहां खो गए और तुम्हारी यादों में ये चाय ही मेरा सुकून बनकर रह गया। कहते हैं ना कि किसी के जाने के बाद ही उसकी पसंद और अहमियत समझ आती है।आज देखो तो तुम्हारे जाने के बाद ये कॉफी बेसुकूनी और चाय सुकून बन गई।

तुम्हारी......

Shivansh Sharma

He is Shivansh Sharma. Basically, from Indore but perusing MBA (Marketing &Hr) in Mysore Karnataka. He always has a passion for writing the thoughts which come into his mind. A hardcore foodie as he belongs to Indore. He is the one who is always ready to help his near ones. His life revolves around his family and friends. He is always self -motivated, enthusiastic and a person with positive vibes. He is a ceauthor of 20+ books and a compiler of 1 book. currently holding the position of Project Coordinator in Flairs and Glairs. His only belief is just to live happily and enjoy every moment of life. You can contact him on ig@shivanshrockzzzzz

चाय और तुम

सुनो चलो आज बयां करते है ,
तुम्हारी और मेरी चाय की बाते,
वो हमारा चाय पे मिलना ,
तुम्हारा वो दोस्तों को बहाना बनाकर आना,
कॉलेज लाइब्रेरी का बोलकर ,
कॉलेज के बाहर टपरी पर आना,
और आकर मुझे डांटना ,
और फिर चाय देखकर
अपना गुस्सा भूल जाना ,
और फिर अपनी चाय पे चर्चा करना ,
और फिर जानमुझकर बस छोड़ना,
और फिर घर छोड़ने का हुकुम देना ,
फिर एक कप चाय और लेकर बैठ जाना,
कभी शकर काम होने पर ,
 तो कभी अदरक कम होने पर ,
चाय वाले से लड़जाना ,
और फिर मेरा तुम्हे चाय का
कप पकड़े तुम्हे मनाना,
और क्या तुम्हे याद है
जब मैने पहली बार तुम्हारे लिए
चाय बनाई थी अपने घर पर ,
और तुम्हारा चाय की तारीफ करना ,
वो दो कप चाय और तुम्हारा मेरे पास होना ,
और फिर मेरा तुम्हे देखते देखते ,
चाय भूल तुम्हारी बातों में खो जाना ,
और चाय पे घंटो तुम्हारे साथ बकवास करना ,
वो चाय के साथ हमारे खास पल,

जहां हमें दुनिया की परवाह नहीं थी,
बस एक दूसरे की बाते सुनते रहते ,
बस चाय के बहाने ,
तुमसे करते मुलाकाते,
वो चाय की चुस्कियों में तुम्हारा साथ,
भले अब साथ नहीं है ,
पर चाय पे हुई बाते याद आज भी है ,
चलो आज फिर चाय पीते है ,
बस फर्क इतना है की
तुम किसी और के साथ पिओगे
और हम अकेले बैठे चाय की चुस्की लेंगे।।

Dr Rakesh R Mund

Dr Rakesh R Mund has been participating in more than 150 anthology and his solo books are ishq -e-panhi & Vidhwansh available on amazon, flipkart and others platform. He is winner of Omg Book Of Records. He read veda and diffrent literatures which give a glimpse on his writing. You can contact with him: insta- Rakeshmundr_

तेरे बिन अधूरी जिंदगी

साथ रहते थे सब साथ छोडे आज
कुछ बताना है साथ दिया जो वही राज़ ।
बैशाख से लेकर बसंत तक हर पल वही
सिर्फ चाय नहीं चाय बिन अधूरी जिंदगी यहीं ।।
एक ऐसा नशा जो जोडकर बना बंदगी
सच यही है तेरे बिन अधूरी जिंदगी ।।१।।
मौसम बदला मेहबूब बदला बदला जहाँ
तुझसा दोस्थ ही खुशी और ग़म तु रहे वहाँ ।
इनसान भूला इनसानियत लेकिन तु भूला नहीं
चुस्कियों से मन भर देता तेरे लिए कुछ गिला नहीं ।।
हमेशा था और रहेगा हर पल बस यही तिश्रगी
सच यही है तेरे बिन अधूरी जिंदगी ।।२।।

Jaspreet Kaur

Jaspreet Kaur is a writer and a poet. She is good at conveying philosophical ideas and best known for writing motivational and romantic poetry. Proud co-author of 20+ anthologies. Life is full of sweet and sour experiences which she
loves to depict in form of poetry. You can follow her journey on Instagram @inkked_solace_
@_kaur_jaspreet_

चाय और वो मुलाकात

उस इश्क़ की शुरुआत थी
बात वो कुछ ऐसे खास थी
चाय पर हुई जो मुलाकात थी
दो दिलों का वो राज़ थी
पहली नज़र वो जादू कर गई
बातें हुई जो दिल को छू गई
हशर ये हुआ कि आदत हो गई
चाय की और दीदार ए यार की

इत्तेफ़ाक़ था वो या संजोग कोई
जो हुआ वो एक ख्वाब सा था
एक पल में ज़िन्दगी बदल गई
एक नया सिलसिला हुआ शुरू था
बदले रंग ज़माना बदल गया
नहीं बदला तो वो जुनून इश्क़ का
एक कहानी सा लगता है सुनने में
जो किया बयान हकीकत का किस्सा था

चाय - ज़रूरत ज़िन्दगी की

दिन भर की थकान को
चाय की वो चुस्की चुरा लेती है
एक नई ताज़गी का एहसास भी
एक पल में करा देती है
उदास चेहरे पर चाय की प्याली
मुस्कुराहट बिखेर जाती है
इसके बिना शुरुआत दिन की
अधूरेपन में बदल जाती है
बंद दिमाग को खोलने में
जो पूरा साथ निभाती है
नींद आंखों से चुराने का
हुनर बेहतरीन ये जानती है
एक एक करके जाने कितनों की
जुबान पर छोड़ असर ये जाती है
ज़रूरत ज़िन्दगी की कहते है लोग
नाम जिसका चाय जादुई दवाई है

Kirti Goel

Hello Readers!
She is Kirti Goel. A medical professional soaked in the love of poetry. She believes everyone has something special that needs to be explored. She explored her inner self & got gifted by the galaxy of words inside her. She is a co-author of many anthologies including the Record aiming book "India Needs A Change", 3AM Thoughts, when they smile, Kuch Tou Log Kahenge & many more.
Through her nib, she inks the reality of life and expresses her true self. She believes all we need is a heart to write & words to express.
You can reach out to her musings on Instagram
@Poetryy_Fair
For her readers, she wanted to say:
"There is always a story to begin"
So, buckle up your laces and write your Life Story Yourself!!

चाय की टपरी

तुम आ कर देख लो
बैठें है आज भी वही
बुत बन कर यादों में तेरी,
जिन गलियों में हमारे
इश्क़ के चर्चे थे कभी।

जहां पनपा हमारा प्यार था
उस "चाय की मिठास" सा
जहां सिर्फ तेरे होने से
महक जाता था समां...
ठीक वैसे ही आज भी, तेरे नाम से
महक जाता है 'इलायची' सा
उस चाय की टपरी का समां !!

हां, आज भी हैं हम वही खड़े
इंतजार में तेरे...
उस चाय की टपरी के संग
एकटक तकते तुम्हे ...

चाय की चुस्की

अगर एक चाय मिल जाए
वो गर्म कुल्हड़ में
मां के हाथ का प्यार मिल जाए
कुटी हुई अदरक और इलायची के रंग भर से ही
सर्द हवाओं में सुकून मिल जाएं।

जो देती हैं हमको आराम
उतार देती हैं हमारे दिनभर की थकान
जिसके आगे फीके है ज़ाम
अम्मा! तेरे हाथ की बनी
"चाय की चुस्की" है उसका नाम!!

Ronak Jain

रौनक जैन ख़्वाजा की नगरी अजमेर से आते हैं। इन्हें कविता, कहानी एवं ग़ज़लों से अपार स्नेह है। रोज़ कुछ नया सीखने, जानने व अलग-अलग लोगों से जान-पहचान करने का व्यक्तित्व रखते हैं। अपनी भावनाओं को कविताओं का रूप देना इन्हें अत्यंत प्रिय है। अपने उपनाम में 'Janaab ...#' का प्रयोग करते हैं जो इनकी रचनाओं को एक अलग पहचान देती है। आप अनेकों लेखक-समूहों से जुड़े हैं एवं साहित्य के प्रचार में अपना योगदान दे रहे हैं। इस संकलन का पात्र बनकर काफ़ी उत्साहित एवं अपनी लेखन शैली को और सुदृढ़ करने हेतु कर्मशील हैं।

~ एक मुलाक़ात ~

एक रोज़ चाय पर बुलाएंगे तुम्हें,
हर राज़ ज़हन के बताएंगे तुम्हें।
ख़ामोश हो चुकी इस जुबान का फर्क,
चाय की चुस्की के साथ सुनाएंगे तुम्हें।

बारिश की कुछ बूँदें होंगी,
कुछ क़शमक़श शायद हमारा दिल भी झेले,
कुछ अतीत की बातें होंगी,
कुछ बिसरे अरमानों के मेले।
मेरा हर जख़्म तुम्हारी छुअन चाहेगा,
हर टूटा स्वप्न तुम्हें भी जब याद आएगा,
पर शायद तब हमारे बीच ये खुमारी ना होगी,
दो घूँट चाय के बीच कोई जुबानी ना होगी।

ताज़े जख़्म जलते बहुत हैं,
थोड़े पुराने दुखते बहुत हैं,
निशान जो छोड़ जाते हैं ज़हन में,
अक्सर वो किस्से चुभते बहुत हैं।

एकाएक तुम्हारा हाथ थाम लूँगा मैं,
बात तुम्हारे मन की जब भाप लूँगा मैं,
पोंछ लेंगे आँसू अपने उस एक पल में हम,
तुम मेरा लो और तुम्हारा नाम लूँगा मैं।
हँस कर बातें सारी, ठंडी चाय के साथ किनारे रखना,
कुछ पल ख़ामोशी और बस आँखों में तकना,
बदले हमारे रास्तों को याद कर के चटपटे किस्से चखना,
फिर भी एक दूजे से पल भर के लिए भी ना थकना।

एक घंटी फ़ोन की फिर हमें जगाएगी,
मुलाकात शायद ये भी अधूरी रह जाएगी,
तुम मन मसोस कर अलविदा जब कहोगी,
नज़रें अपनी भाषा में बिछड़ने का दर्द कह जाएगी।

एक ख़त धीरे से तुम्हारे पर्स में मैं सरका दूँगा,
एक चिट्ठी तुम मेरे नाम बताते जाना,
जो मुकम्मल ना हुई मोहब्बत तो क्या ?
दोस्ती की कुछ रस्में तुम निभाते जाना।
जाते-जाते एक बार पीछे मुड़ के देखना,
नम आँखों से पर्स तुम्हारा सोफे पर टेकना,
भागकर मेरी बाहों में, एक उम्र के लिए समा जाना,
मेरी महक को अपने भीतर हमेशा के लिए रमा जाना।

मन में सुकून की लहर दौड़ेगी,
हँसी और झूठे नकाबों की मोहताज ना रहे,
तुम निखर जाओगी इतना,
जैसे दिल की कोई सूनी दराज़ खोल आए।

Kuldeep Sharma

Kuldeep Sharma is a civil engineer pass out from Medicap's Institute of Indore Madhya Pradesh. He is working as a Poet, Writer past two years. He is also interested in Painting, Drawing. He follows many writer and poet but the favorite one is Jaun Elia and Gulzar. He wants to be a fine writer and fulfill his dream as a writer.

Ishq Cha...

उन्होंने पूछा चाय पियोगे?
अब चाय कि कौन मना करता है साहब
और फिर पूछने वाले वो हों,
तो ज़हर भी पेस कर दीजिये.

जो हमने कहा हाँ पिएंगे,
उन्होंने तपाक से कहा,
दो बना लो!
हमारे लिये कुछ नया न था,
हमने चाय पेस की.

कप को जो होंठो का स्पर्श मिला
मानो कप खिल उठा,
ज्यों ही चाय उन्होंने पी,
बोले शक़्कर घुली नहीं.

हाल ए दिल हमने भी बयां कुछ यूँ किया,
जाने के बाद आपके,
न चाय में शक़्कर पसंद रही
और न ज़िन्दगी में रही मिठास.

क्या सोचते हो ज़नाब चाय भी इक इश्क़ है

Janeman

Tu chai ki piyali

mai coffee ki taan

Everyone loves you because

chai hai sabki jaan.

अभय कुमार

अभय कुमार रिटेल ब्रांड में लगभग 10 वर्षों से स्टोर मैनेजर हैं। वह स्वभाव से कवि हैं और दिन-प्रतिदिन के अपने अनुभवों को लिखने के लिए उपयोग करते हैं। अभय शब्द के खेल से प्यार करते हैं और नए शब्द सीखने की कोशिश करते हैं।

जैसा कि उन्हें एक प्रेम विवाह का आशीर्वाद मिला है, उनके पास प्यार के बारे में लिखने के लिए बहुत कुछ है और एक संयुक्त परिवार उन्हें परिवार के बारे में लिखने में मदद करता है।

<u>चाय और तुम</u>

सर्दी की सुबह का तुम्हारा आलिंगन
जिस तरह सकून दे जाता है,
एक प्याली चाय को भी
ये हुनर खूब आता है,
रात की गहराइयों के बाद आँख खुलते ही
जिनका मुझे इंतजार है,
उनमें से एक तुम हो
और एक चाय है,
बहुत कुछ एक जैसा है
मेरे यार में मेरी चाय में,
दोनों बहुत जरूरी हैं
मेरे हृदय में, मेरे निकाय में,
कुछ बातों पर गौर करूँ तो
तुम बिलकुल वैसी हो,
अरे यकीन तो करो मेरा
तुम बिलकुल चाय जैसी हो,
रंग सांवला मेरी चाय का
रंग साँवरा तेरा,
मैं दीवाना उसका
मैं बावरा हूँ तेरा,
उसकी मिठास मेरे होठों पर
तेरी मिठास है दिल में,
कुछ तो अधूरा रह जाता है
दोनों के बिना महफ़िल में,
उसकी वो भीनी खुशबू
उसकी वो गरमाहट,
जीवन में ऐसे जैसे
तुम्हारे आने की आहट,

वो मनमोहक, तुम मनभावन
वो बारिश सुर्ख़ धरातल पर, तुम मेरे दिल का सावन,
वो लत, तुम नशा हो
वो मोहब्बत, तुम वफ़ा हो
वो मेहनत, तुम किस्मत हो
वो मददगार, तुम रेहमत हो
वो ज़ायक़ेदार, तुम स्वाद हो
वो इच्छा, तुम जज़्बात हो
वो आशिक़ी, तुम बन्दगी हो
पर यकीनन तुम दोनों मेरी ज़िन्दगी हो!!

मैं जानता हूँ, वो हमेशा तुम्हारे लिए
एक सौतन सी रही है,
पर आओ न दो पल पास बैठो मेरे
मैंने चाय चढ़ा रखी है,
और खूब जमेगा रंग वहां
जहाँ हम तीनों मिल जाएँ,
एक मैं, एक तुम
और एक हमारी चाय!!

Rohan "Vikramaditya"

Rohan is currently living in Lucknow and is 18 years old. He is an Ex - Kvian, and an aspiring engineer. Keeping " Vikramaditya" as his pen name, he always writes to express his own and the ideology of the modern society and have dreams to become a kalamkaar, to shape his future with the tip of his pen, his mightiest weapon. His main interests include writing poetries, singing, playing guitar, cooking, and a spark of gaming along with coding on computer. You can contact him via Email: rohankumarkhare@gmail.com.
Instagram - @rv_kalamkaar. Stay Safe, Enjoy reading!!!

"That Missing Essence"

That one single missing essence,
Missing from each morning's wake up tea,
Leaving thoughts in my mind of its importance,
No one else, but You….

The one best known,
To make me smile and forget all negativity,
And hold my hand and spread only positivity,
Around me, no one else, but You….

The one without whom each day's first sip,
Always felt strange, irritating, making me miss that vibe, that trip,
Adding thoughts in my mind, "Should I call? Should I text?",
No one else, but You….

That one person who corrected me & my mistakes,
Said all the truth & stood with me, whatever it takes,
Just like the burning sip of tea, but great relaxation to the throat,
No one else, but You….

The one whose thoughts I wanted to be a part of,
'Coz of all the beautiful memories she gave me,
And I, in return tried to do the same, but wasn't enough,
No one else, but you….

That one single missing essence,
Whom no one can remove & neither I, can miss its presence,
The one who stays, always with my heart,
Always soothing it, no one else, but You….

"Addicted to Both"

Without any confusion or doubt, I can say,
That I'm addicted to both, you and tea,
Both, makes my world look real, cures my day,
Minimizing all my pain, and understanding all my plea….

Tea, the tonic, the more its strong,
The more clutter, it clears away from my mind,
Freshens me up, prepares me for ahead,
All the tasks, and all the grind….

You, my strength, the "one" who understands my heart,
Support all my decisions, stand with me all the time,
The person without whom my day never completes,
Whose one text excites, and someone I can't deceit…

When stuck, my thoughts always visit the same spot to roost,
Tea & you for releasing all stress, and giving me a much   -
needed boost,
Sometimes tea make me nostalgic, reminding all old
memories,
The best time spent with my family and you, making me
smile….

It's you who protect me from all the threats,
And take care of me like no one else,
Of course, thanks would be too small for what you do,
But I love you more than anyone in this world…

Yes, I am addicted, to both of you,
And this addiction is sweet, needed and non – harmful too,
'Coz many met and went, no one stayed,
But you both, my constants, never asked to go away

Sheetal Ahuja

Sheetal Ahuja is the blessed daughter of Almighty, Loving Caring Parents taught by mighty mentors living in the aura of fun-loving inspiring buddies and an aspiring author. She is the proud resident of village Saniana of district Fatehabad, Haryana and has completed her post-graduation in Chemistry from ChaudharyDeviLal University, Sirsa. Writer has enthusiastically participated in Interzonal Literary Youth Festival,organized by KUK University and also a participant under various poetry competitions like Wi ngword Poetry Competition.She creatively owns the Facebook page Poetry door@AsD and invites fellow readers to dive deep down in the melting ocean of emotions of love,care and affection.

Hmari Haseen Shaam.

Arma hai ek dil me mere gujar lu kucch pal sang tere,Vo pal
jisme na office,na files na ghar ka koi kaam ho ,saath tere jo
beete aisi ek hasee shaam ho.Beshumar baatein ho kucch
ansuni kucch ankahi,
Garma Garm Chai ki chuskia ho sana ho jisme pyar vala
masala vahi
Sondhi mitti ki khushboo or tip-tip barsat ho,
Bageeche ke jhulo par nayaab palo ka saath ho.
Mahobbat se parosu mai tumhe chai ki pyaali,kyuki tum khaas
ho,Tum rafta rafta bharna ghoont uski jisme ishq -ae-mithaas
ho
Do pal toh jrra nikaalo jisme sukoo aaram   ho, do tum kaho
apni or do suno hmaari baaki sab kucch viraam ho.
Kyunki Snjo lena chaahti hu mai vo har lamha ,vo ishq me
dooba yaadon ka jaam ,Jisme ho Sondhi Mitti Ki
Khushboo,TipTip Barsaat,Do Cup Masala Chai,
Hum Tum or Sirf Hmari Hasee Shaam.

Sham-Ae-Ishq Hajoori.
(A Romantic Reply To Hmari Haseen Shaam)

Arma toh iss dil me bhi hai kucch aisa or kyu na ho jab sanam ho tere jaisa.

Jald hi aaenge voh pal jisme na office na files na ghar ka koi kaam hoga.Anginat barkaton ka Jashn Sare Sam hoga.

Beshak hongi kucch ans uni kucch ankahi baatein,kyunki jannat si khoobsurat hogi hmaari mulakaate.

Or hongi Garma Garm Chai ki chuskia Pyaar vaale masale se dil hoga ishqia.

Sondhi Mitti ki khushboo or tiptip barsaat hogi,Bageecho ke jhulo par nayaab Din-O-Raat Hogi.

Mahobbat se parosana tum mujhe chai ki pyali ,taaki reh na jaaye koi hasrat bhi khaali. Pakodo si teekhi imli ki khatti meethi hmaari har yaad hogi,basa skogi jo apne man me vo khubsoorat fir milne ki fariyaad hogi.

Mai rafta rafta bharunga ghoont uski jis   me ishq -ae-mithaas hogi,or alfaazo me samet lunga mehsoos krne ko jab bhi tum paas na hogi.

Do pal hmari mahobbat ke jald hi aaenge Chai ki chuskio sang dil ke taraane gaaenge, Kyuki us pal me vo sukoon vo aaram hoga jb na office na files na ghar ka koi kaam hoga.

Snjo lena jee bharke vohar pal, vo ishq me dooba yaadon ka jaam,Jisme hogi Sondhi Mitti ki Khushboo,TipTip Barsaat ,Do Cup Masala Chai,Hum Tum Or Sirf Hmari Hasee Shaam

.

Mansvi Kathiriya

I'm 21 years old ambitious girl. I have completed my bachelor of science in botany subject. I love to read novels. I'm not professional writer but writing is one of my hobbies. I have inspired by nirmika sigh and gulzar. I write thoughts through my feelings.

तुम और चाय.

मेरी जिंदगी की दो चाहत ,
कोई उसे जरूरत कहता है तो कोई उसे आदत
लेकिन मेरे लिए मेरी जिंदगी का हिस्सा है,
और इसी से मेरी जिंदगी का वजूद भी..
ना कभी उन्हें में छोड़ पाऊँगी ना कभी मैं उन्हें छोड़ने के बारे में
सोच पाऊँगी...
क्योंकि उनका जो नशा है वह मेरी आंखों में है, और उसका
एहसास मेरे सीने में है ।
चाय से मेरी हर सुबह होती है वहीं सुबह हसीन तुमसे है ।
तुम दोनो से मेरी हर शाम होती है ओर रंगीन भी ...
तुम्हारा नशा मेरे रूह में इस कदर उतरा है
तुम्हारे बिना मेरी हर सुबह और शाम अधूरी है
न जाने कब ये चाहत हकीकत होगी,
एक चाय और एक तुम हर शाम मेरे साथ होगे।

(2)

मुस्कुराहट तुम्हारी हो और वजह हम बने .
तकलीफ़ तुम्हारी हो और आसूँ हमारे बहे.
गलती तुम्हारी हो और मुहताज हम बने.
आखिर में,
महोब्बत तुम्हारी हो और उसके हकदार सिर्फ हम बने।

Sushmita Mishra

A teacher and youtuber with multi skills.
लखनवी अंदाज़ के साथ संगम का प्रवाह..
आसमां छूने की चाहत है पर जमीं से दूर नहीं जाऊंगी
हौसला गर टूटा तो फिर नयी राह बनाऊंगी
ग़म तो बहुत हैं दुनिया में इनसे दूर कहाँ जाऊंगी
पर ज़िन्दगी थोड़ी ही है तो हंस के ही बिताउंगी..

<u>चाय और तुम</u>

वो घर के पास वाला नुक्कड़
मेरे घर की खिड़की और उसकी तिरछी नज़र
कितने अच्छे थे ना वो प्यार के शुरुआती पल
वो सर्दियों के शाम
खिड़की से झाँकती मैं
वो कुल्हड़ वाली स्पेशल चाय और
तुमको याद करती मै...

दिनों दिन बढ़ती वो मुलाकात
तुम्हारा नुक्कड़ पर आना और मेरा खिड़की पर इंतज़ार
धीरे -धीरे चाय के रंग सा गहराता अपना प्यार
वो सर्दियों की शाम
इंतज़ार में बैठी मैं
वो कुल्हड़ वाली स्पेशल चाय और
तुमको याद करती मै...

अब तो सिलसिलेवार होने लगी बात
कुछ खट्टी कुछ मीठी सी जीवन की हर शाम
सपने नए सुहाने फिर पलकें लायी नींद के साथ
वो सर्दियों की शाम
तकिये से लिपटती मैं
वो कुल्हड़ वाली स्पेशल चाय और
तुमको याद करती मै...

पर ठहरा कहाँ है वक़्त पीछे छूटी सारी याद
जो तुम्हें खुशी दे ऐसी लम्बी कब होती है रात
जैसे ठंड में जलती लकड़ियों की बच गयी थोड़ी राख
वो सर्दियों की शाम

और राख समेटती मैं
वो कुल्हड़ वाली स्पेशल चाय और
तुमको याद करती मै...

Maniska Das

As an amateur writer she wants to travel the writing world while collecting inspirations and remarking them by her words. She'd already published her work in many Anthologies and still dream big. Belonging to the holy city Puri Odisha India she scripts by heart and develop it to be explored. With million hopes, she takes all the smile by the ink of her pen.

यादों के कुछ पल

शर्दियों के वो दिन,
बाहर थंद और खायलों में तुम,
हाथों में इक गरम चाय
और सुबह की बात बन जाए।

इन रातों को पता है सपनो के राज़,
सिर्फ दिल ही जाने वो किस्का ताज,
अरे अभि को तूम्हारे साथ पुरी शाम बितानी है,
चाय बिस्कुट के साथ बचपन की कहानी जो सुनानि है।

कॉलेज के वो दिन तो   की टपरी पर बीत गये,
दोस्तो के साथ वो हर मैदान जीत गये,
अब बस यादों के सहारे ये आंखें हैं नम,
ज़िन्दगी की इस भाग दौड़ मैं कहाँ गुम होगये हम?

रोज़ की तरह आज एक खुसनुमार सा सपना फिर टूट गया,
सुबह होते ही पेपर के साथ एक कप चाय और मिल गया,
बरसों पुराना देखा ख्वाब सच होके सामने बैठा था,
क्यों न आज फिर उस सपने में वापस चले साथ?

(2)

"आपके इनायत में ये दिल कुर्बान है,
आपके नज़रों में ढली सुबह शाम है,
आपके नरम हाथों की वो चाय भी गरम है,
अरे किस्मत की हवा तो यूंही बदनाम है।"

Khushi Agrawal

Khushi Agrawal is 20 -year-old girl living in Fort -Songadh, Gujarat. She is B.tech ICT student.

She is co-author in 20+ anthology, including record holding anthology.

She is compiler of 5+ anthology.

She likes reading fiction novels and autobiography. Her ambition is to crack UPSC CSE exams.

You can join her on khushi2712.ka@gmail.com.

IG @a. khushi2704

Ek Khubsurat Subha!

Aap ,Mein Aur Aapke hatho ki bani woh chai,
Bas yahi Vajah hai meri bhagvan se har raat Ek nayi subha ki
guzarish karne ki.
Aapka yun mujhe pyaar se subha subha jagana,
Phir apne hatho se bani woh chai ka cup mere hatho mein
thamana,
Aur har roz, yeh saval "Theek bani hai na, Jaisi Tumhe
pasand hai waisi hi hai na?"
Jaise mere dil ko baag baag kar jata hai
Baar baar mera dil shukariya karta hai uss uperwale ka jisne
aapko meri zindagi mein bheja hai.
Mera mann bass yahi chahta hai
yeh waqt yahi tham jaye aur hum teeno yani AAP Mein Aur
Aapke Hatho Ki Bani Chai bass yuhi humeha sath reh jayee.

Agrima Viraj

She is a student who has passed her 12th grade in the year 2020 and is currently preparing for the competitive exam NEET. Apart from dreaming to get the prefix of a 'Doctor' before her name, she is also passionate about writing down her thoughts and emotions to give them a devise of poetry. Her writings generally mound out the teenage fantasy, dreams, rage, lifestyle, insight , delusions, etc. She can very well portray herself to the readers via her writings.

To get in touch with more of her works, refer to the following:

Instagram: @agrima_viraj

YourQuote: Agrima Viraj

Wordpress: theuntouchedmind.wordpress.com

Mail id: agrimav.hyd@gmail.com

ज़ायका प्यार का

शाम के कुछ बजे थे सात
और तुम थे वहाँ मेरे साथ
मेज़ पर रखी थी दो गिलास
कहने को था कुछ ना खास

उस चाय से वो निकलती भाप
और मेरे ठंडे काँपते हुए हाथ
मेरा सामने तुम्हारा खिला सा चेहरा
आँखें जिसकी देती मेरे मन को पहरा

पहले ही घूंट के साथ जो मिला सुकून
ऐसे ऐहसास का मुझे कहाँ था मालूम
तुम्हारी दिलकश बातें और मेरी मुस्कान
लगता था चाय में घुलते शक्कर के समान

तुम्हारा मेरे कंधे पर सर रख कर सोना
लगता मानो इलायची-गुड़ का एक होना
हर दिन तुमसे बात करना लगता जैसे
चाय के लिए होता हर पल एक ख़ुमार

कुछ अनोखा सा लगता है वो मिजाज़
होता जिससे तुमसे प्यार का आगाज़
बयाँ करने को बचते ना कोई अलफाज़
कि कितने ज़रूरी हो तुम मेरे सरताज

चाय का ज़ायका हो या तुमसे प्यार
दोनो का ही होता है बेसब्री से इंतज़ार

Rinitha Priya J

Rinitha Priya,
a final year P.G student in English literature. She is a writer
and singer. she is good in writing poems which shows the
importance of love. She has an intense passion in books. She
is a young writer who has stepped into the world of writing.

Love of My Life

You & I have been the perfect partners
Whenever I'm in delight, I think of you
Whenever I'm in a rage, I need you
Whenever I'm confused, you make me clear
Whenever I'm lost, you bring me back.

There is something in you that attracts me
Your fragrance takes me to another world
When you give me a deep sweet kiss, your flavour takes my
stress away
Your aroma makes me kiss you with my sip.

My day starts & end with you
You help me to connect with many people
You are the source of my happiness
Without you my day become the nastiest.

You are my best travel partner
 You are always my energy booster
I will never give up on you
The world calls you 'Tea"
But you are always the Love of My Life...!

Ananya Mohanty

Ananya Mohanty hailing from the city of Rairangpur. An author in 60+ anthologies and a compiler also. She is also Kalam world record holder and Spectrum Inspiring Indian Women record holder. And currently a manuscript maker at The Opus Coliseum. Writing is like a way to say your feelings out. So, I write to express myself. So, some of the writings are in real my own stories. My life My story. I love writing for myself. This is also something I wrote from some of my life phase. My much of the w   ritings are on romance, mystery, fantasy, motivation and horror.

The Tea Lovers

It all started 4 years ago with the as usual busy day with classes and work. It was the time when we were in college pursuing our dreams, enjoying our live and having fun with friends. As usual I went for my tea to start my day with the taste and aroma of it and one boy came and asked for it too at the same time but to our luck, we only have one last cup left in the cafe and we both smiled at each other and asked the waiter to give us an empty cup and we both divided it into half and started enjoying our drink with some formal introduction and came to know that we both are from same class and section too. After our sweet intro we both made our way to class and sat near each other as we both don't have any friends to be with. As I am a simple loner type girl and he is very free frank boy so it's kind of like we both somehow like each other company and presence. It kind of felt strange at first but I felt like it's not a coincidence.

From that day on we both spent most of our time with each other and we both eventually came to know that we both belong to same homeland and live-in opposite neighborhood. We both felt a unique spark with each other like we both are made for each other. But as saying goes by "If you need something, you need to lose something." same thing happened with us too specially with me.

One day we were chattering about random topic and suddenly a girl came and hugged him from out of the blue. And he became shocked and was about to push her away when she called him as "Panda I miss you." and he widened his eyes and smiled widely and hugged her even more. I was just standing there trying to understand the situation and after a good 5 minutes they noticed my presence and he introduced her as his best friend but she cut him off and added as his ex-too. I just

gave them a fake smile and introduced myself and that girl just gave me a look like 'let's see what we have got here, smirk'. and as my habit I ignored her.

From that day onwards that girl was like an annoying old lady between us. She neve r let us have those happy conversation and rather than that just try to boast around about her clothes, makeup, her character and all and to be honest it was irritating and one day I decided to have fun with her a little. As the classes of that was coming to an end and the luck was on my side because the professor had given her the task to collect the project and submit to him and thats my chance as I held his hand and our both bags and ran out of the college to the park. After reaching there we both looked   at each other for some second and burst into laughter and sat down on a bench. It was a calm weather with some couple chattering and children playing and giggling and suddenly the scent of tea hit both of our nostrils and a smile made its way on our facesWe grabbed two loving cup of tea and enjoyed the calm silence. After sometime he broke the silence saying its already late and we should go back home and after sometime we bid our goodbyes and went to our dorms.

After this we both always find a way to be away from her and be with each other like we used to be and slowly we became more closer to each other. But suddenly he vanished from everywhere before my birthday and I was sad and upset as where he went to without informing me.

On the day of my birthday, I received a text from him saying "Meet me at the place we met first at 5 O'clock, And wear the dress kept under your door.", reading his text I blushed a little and happily went to take the dress and it was a simple white frock with blue floral prints on it, just the way I like.

After getting ready I went to the cafeteria where we first met but the whole cafe was dark and I called his name and suddenly all the lights went on with everyone singing happy birthday song and there he was, the man with w hom I am in love with. And he hugged me and wished me happy birthday and we cut the cake and he asked me to close my eyes for the gift and I followed his instruction.

After telling me to open my eyes, I was standing there breaking down out of happiness as he was kneeling in front of me holding a tea cup with a paper written as " Will You Be My Tea Lover?" and I just forgot how to speak and just nod my head as a yes and he smiled through his tears and stand up and hold both of my hands and said, " I love youfrom the first met we had, I fell in love with your voice then, then your bubbly nature, your jealous angry bird look, your cute look, your determination to do everything to help others, and finally I fell in love with you for who you are. I Love You."

And it's been 3 years from then and here we are exchanging our vows with each other and promising each other to stay with each other and understand each other and love each other and trust each other till the almighty do us apart.

Now we are each other's tea lover forever and ever.

Ms. Ishrat Jahan Noormohammed Khan

Ms Ishrat jahan khan is a passionate Teacher and a Writer she loves reading and writing. Loving and caring is her hobby. And keep learning and accept the positive suggestion is her quality. She belongs to North India and stays at Ulhasnagar (Maharashtra). Loves humanity always.

चाय और मैं

चाय और मैं
जैसे दोस्त पुराने
साथ है जैसे जमाने
जब मन होता उदास
चाय होती बस पास

मुस्कुराहट बन गई
जिंदगी बन गई
वजह बन गई
बंदगी बन गई
मकान बन गई

चाय के बिना
अधूरा लगता जीना
चार हो या पांच कप
हम पी लेते चाय कप

चाय के लिए लड़ जाए
जो हमसे चाय छुड़ाए
चाय एक नशा बन गई
जीने का हिस्सा बन गई

दिन की सुरूवात चाय
दिन की अंत चाय
ऑफिस की स्ट्रैस तो चाय
मैन उदास तो चाय
भाई अब बस
चाय और मै
बस हम दोनों

(2)

Tea is life
Tea is life
Just one sip
And the tension is zip

Tea is smile
At far away and mile
Tea lover has style
So, don't be fragile

Hitesha Sahani

Just a teen wondering the world

(1)

Our meeting: Today I was just remembering the day I met you. i guess that was the best day of my life, After the day you became my second love first was still tea. You came to my life when I was going through the worse, your importance is much more than what can I even describe. I remember the first thing I loved about you was that you also love to drink tea I know that was awkward as I was already in love with you but that moment you made me love you even more. Our first date when I forget to bring a rose and the wholetime, I was searching for it. I regret we are not together now maybe we are meant to be separated but truly saying every time I make tea I think of you I remember whenever I'm angry with you, you always used to make tea for me and we both forget the whole world and just enjoy our tea with lots of gossips. who knows you also think of me but that's not worthynow, I guess? Now I can say I loved tea but not more than you. Just a hope we'll meet again someday

Lingampally Pradeep Reddy

Pradeep is an engineer who wants to write his thoughts without a filter of societal limitations.

(1)

Dear chai,

I know you since I was a little child. I always enjoy the aroma of fresh tea brewed once in the morning and once in the evening as well. You are my confidence booster, stress relaxer, mood changer and my simple, constant and first solution to every problem. You become my doctor when the headache is storming. You become my motivator and push me when I feel like giving up. You become my alarm in the late nights to wake me up when I fall asleep. You taught me hospitality by offering tea to every guest who visited and rejecting tea as a guest mean social insult. you brighten up both the cold and rainy season, in spring it becomes poetry. you make my health better, with your mood swings called that extr a added black comedy, masala, or your natural beauty green.
Consuming tea helped me with focus during meditation, which promotes relaxation and reduces anxiety, helped to calm the wandering mind and improves alertness to prevent sleep.
The tradition of dri nking tea was considered a way of nourishing and purifying the body on a deeper level. I ask my friends to enjoy it, appreciate the aroma, and drink it so that wandering thoughts are restrained, friendships are strengthened, and manners and virtue are cultivated.

you have a positive solution for every tough question. A day without is unimaginable. Thank you for staying in my life.

Regards,
wanderer.

Mehak Bhan

Mehak bhan, living in budgam district of kashmir, learner and had played many national level tournaments. (national player of kho_ kho). I am a deep thinker and a keen observer, a worshiper of words. I love to read poems of many legendary poets like "Rumi".I do explore new places and cuisine sometimes. I never really dislike anything but I often failed to understand the hearts of the people that never carry kindness within. I strongly trust the goodness and humbleness of ones.

"Chai aur Tum".

You are just like the tea which I can sip and can feel the true bond, true affection and true intimacy. I got known whenever I may have trouble, you are the one who fills my cup of tea that I sip and feel the internal peace within.

You are the one who teaches me life is like a cup of tea "it is all about how the taste is".

(Here you got a hot tea if you sip it soon your tongue will burn but when you sip it comfortably with peace within, it will cost your inner peace) You are same like the tea, I am addicted to you as you cost my inner peace. You gave many tastes to my life. You taught me you h ave to stand brave in front of your enemies, then your life is worthwhile. As you are gone through this all and experienced enough. You are just like the tea, sweet, peaceful and full of taste of which I am addicted. I wish I will feel your inspiring sweet taste for my entire life.

You are the one who will surely fill up the sorrows of my life with happiness and internal peace like a role of tea, you play the same role in my life as tea plays. You are very beneficial for me because you keep me strong, fresh, energetic; you make me feel stress free whenever I feel stressed.

You are same like the tea as my life begins after tea that is my life begins after you. You are the one who will never change taste for me. You are just like a cup of tea like a cup of peace.

I may thank god you are mine cup of tea!

Our bond is just like a sweet cup of tea!

I may thank god you are mine cup of tea!

A special blend of you and me!

You are just like the melodious taste of a tea that begins with your sensitivity!

You are mine cup of tea which sounds the same like when we stir tea with a spoon!

Thanks for giving full meaning to my life, it is only because
of you!
I can taste my life like I do!
It's only you!
Only you!
My dearest father!
Only you!
(Mehak_bhan)

Rudransh Bhattacharya

Not a professional writer but enroute to become one.
I'm a student and working to get my ways straight, still learning and figuring out ways of life and even a lifetime is less for that. Want to see a day where even   the pain one go through earns him money when someone else reads it and connects through it.

मुख्तलिफ

एक आखरी इबारत फिर उसके नाम,
जिसके साथ बीता करती थी हर सांझ।
रेशम सी चाय पत्ती,
हल्की मिठास कम,
घर हो या टपरी,
लहज़े में नहीं था कोई भ्रम।

समय के साथ लालसा बढ़ती गई,
चाय और तुम, दोनो रूहानियत सी बनती गई।
था एक वो भी अफसाना हमारा,
चाय और तुम, न जाने कब बन गए सहारा।
चाय और कुल्हड़ जैसी बन गई कुरबत,
फिर एक दफा तुमने कर ली कहीं और इबारत।

पिछली आखिरी बार की तरह, फिर लिखा है उसके नाम,
जिसके साथ बीता करती थी हर सांझ।
अगली बार जल्द होएंगे नहीं फना,
खुशी खुशी अलग होने की होने नही देंगे रिवायत।

Black Tea

I was always a tea person,
You were always a coffee gal.
Not only in thoughts,
But even in habits you had to be so dissimilar.

You knew I was ready to be wherever you wanted me to be,
But hold on, only after I had a cup of tea.

God forbid, we always imagined how life without each other,
will be a tragedy.
Now that it's come to be a truth, I'm reluctant enough to accept
the reality.

Only you understood, wh at my mother's cup of tea meant to
me,
A pinch of more sugar, made me go on a happy spree.

Now that only the cup is left,
Between us, there's nothing left to be dealt.
I wonder if you are a tea person now?
I saw you another day, you still beautiful thou.

I was always a tea person,
You were always a coffee gal.
A few years back?
I thought we'll be married now,
Hold on, writing it some other time, I definitely shall.

Sayandeep Patra

A boy from a small town always had a dream of becoming a writer is heading towards to fulfill the dream.

(1)

Jab duniya daru aur sutte ke naashe mein duba hain,
Mein chai ke naasheri hu,
Jab raato ki jam banti hain,
Tab mein subha ke chai ki chuski lagata hu,
Jab das rupay ka woh tiger biscuit chai mein bhigti hain,
Tab ek neya survad hota hain,
Zindagi ke kuch paalo mein,
Tut jane par bhi,
Ek neya survad hota hain,
Jab dard se saar fat ta hain,
Yaah dosto ke saang lamhe bitte hain,
Tab chai ki ek peyali saath hota hain,
Sayad isiliye chai zindagi ke haar palo mein saath rehta hain,
Ki kisi shayar ka shayari ho,
Yaah kisi lekhak ka soch,
Survad to har kisika chai ke saang e hota hain,
Sayad isiliye tarapti hui dhup mein bhi chai pine ka maaza ata
hain,
Jab sardi ka mausam hota hain,
Aur shyam ke bhuk satane lagti hain,
Tab garam samosa aur chai sukoon de jati hain,
Sayad isiliye chai zindagi ka saathi ban jata hain.

(2)

Jaise chai mein shakkar ghul jati hain,
Waise mein tum se jur chuka hu,
Sayad ishq hua hain tumse firse,
Tum puchogi kaise??
Waise hi jaise shakkar ke bina chai adhuri hain,
Jaise ubalti hui paani chai pattiyo ke bina adhuri hain,
Waise hi yeh dil tumhare bina adhuri hain,
Kyunki adhura yeh dil,
Adhura yeh sangsar,
Tum saath raho to lage,
Jaise chai ko mil chuki hain shakkar.

Vishal K R

Meet Vishal K R, a future doctor with a stylus ! You may notice him to be a silent, sober individual, yet the message he deliver makes you explore your inner self. Doesn't express much through speech , pen and paper knows the emotion. Enigmatic personality expressed via literature. Read on to find why .

If interested, write to his mail –
vishnupriya.vishal@gmail.com.
Follow him on Insta - enigma_6001.

Rendezvous With A Cup Of Tea

Rendezvous, tea to accompany.
Speak about events, light refreshing moments!
Away from lamenting, complaining society, a time to pacify my soul and to escape in time.
A potent concoction to calm my nerves, slumbered souls to rejuvenate in a jiffy!
What more to ask for? A monsoon evening, accompanying hot beverage and a companion for a rendezvous. Blessed soul indeed!
Effervescent emotions, humid emotions to embrace! Luminant ambience, candle light to medium my thoughts!
A passive opinion, conveyed by my tea. To warm my garb, sustaining life A rendezvous I desire, with a cup of tea!

My Terrific Day, Tis to Tea!

Tea, a lesson to reach to   mass! A common platform for a layman to debate. Tea shops to accompany   crowds, a refreshing drink to tackle, the frigid weather!
Relax my body, after a long trail, adorned myself with wool I could get my hands upon! Tea sommelier to be complimented indeed. My refreshed day, albeit with challenges. Bushed souls, help yourself with a cup of tea! Comes out in a range to choose - black, green, brick and oolong, anything you name, emotion synonymous to the mellow beverage. Makes me affable, easy to address. Reunited souls, accompanying tea! A bright day to approach, start with tea! Forget my woes, suture my fragmented opinion, to relax my soul, tis to the tea!

Jayati Thakar

Jayati Thakar, a girl who pursued 'Masters in Arts with major English Literature'. She lives in Bhavnagar, a city in Gujarat. She had appeared in three different national and international literary conferences and represented her research work in variety of literary criteria as, Criticism, Feminism, and Cultural Studies. She loves to learn various foreign languages. Deeply in love to roam around the globe, yet not started her journey. She has more powerful sides than the other as emotional and caring for her dear ones. She is skilled at multiple duties at her interests like event handling, teaching, and counseling. Withal she is good at interacting with the people about their problems at her personal interest to study human psychology carved deep within. She has been remained a co-author in more than fifteen anthologies under varies of publications and finally got her first chance to compile an anthology with 'Flairs and Glairs' Publication and pursues for more.

मौसम की पहली बारिश, चाय और वो किस्से

क्या खुबसूरत यादें है वो; जो कभी लम्हे हुआ करतीं थीं,
याद है? तुम्हारा पेहली दफा मुझसे मिलनां, तुम्हारा चाय पीने से
इनकार करना और मेरा तुम्हेँ जबरदस्ती चाय दे जाना!
उस दिन भी काफीं बारिश हुई थी,
युहीं बातों बातों में तुम्हारा इजहार करना की चाय तुम्हे कम ही पसंद
हुआ करतीं थीं पर, उस दिन की चाय का झायका तुम शायद ही
कभी भुल पाओ!

क्या बेहतरीन दिन हुआ करते थे,
जब मिलने की बहोत सी वजह होती थी, पर मिलने के बाद फरमाइश
बस चाय की करते थे,
मुजे याद है! तुम्हारा वो आते ही चाय पीने की ख्वाहिश करना और
कहेना, "पहलें चाय रख आओ, फिर बहोत कुछ है तुम्हे बताने को",
क्या बात हुआ करती थी उस प्यालेभर चाय की; जो दिल के रास्ते यूँ
खोलती थी की तुम्हारा और मेरा एकदुसरे का हो जाना एक तसव्वुर
से कब हकीकत बन जाता, पता ही नहि चलता था!
उन दिनों लम्हे खुशी के हो या गम के, मजिद एक कप चाय ही काफी
हुआ करती थी एकदुसरे के दिलों में झाँकने के लिए!

तुम्हारा बास्केटबॉल मेच में से जितकर लौटना,
तुम्हारा वो इंटरनेशनल फर्म में एक अच्छी सी पोस्ट पर सिलेक्शन
होना,
तुम्हारा पहेला प्रमोसन हो या कोई और तरक्की, बात सिर्फ़ उस एक
कप चाय से बनतीं, और हर दफा खुशियों की वजह बढती ही चलीं
जाती!

आज सालों गुज़र गये और बीलकुल वैसी ही बारिश हो रहीं हैं

मैं वैसे ही तुम्हारे लौटने का इन्तजार करती हूँ, जैसे पहेले किया करती थी!

पर शायद आज सिर्फ मैं हूँ यहा और ये एक कप चाय, और कुछ पुरानी यादें,

कहेते है गुजरे हुए लम्हे कभी लौटकर नहीं आतें, पर ये वो छाप छोड़ जातें हैं, जो उन लम्हों को दिलों मे हंमेशा ताजा रखती है!

Flairs and Glairs, a platform by a student for the students. We are esteemed youth struggling to carve out our path for our future and we follow a basic mindset Since everyone is not born with allround skills. Joining hands with people who are born to execute it with perfection is the best way to evol ve. Self-Evolution is the need of the hour but, evolving as a community is what we strive for. The initiative as kickstarted by, Founder - Mr. Shubham Shah with the motive to utilize the skillset and talent of writing has now a team of 10+ people who are actively participating into newer forms of learning and discovering talents among youngsters. We Provide platform and services like Publishing opportunities, Open mics, Workshops, Hands-on training. Operating with Brand Name of Flairs and Glairs (Publication House), we offer the chance of elevating a passionate writer to an esteemed author With Brand name Teekhe Zasbaaat. We bring to you an opportunity to get accustomed with the Public Speaking and Presenting of Thoughts along with regular challen ges to brush up your inking spirit. The newest initiative to extend our services we introduced in a new writing Platform- The Glittering Fables and Ink Over Tears.

We Choose to Fly Like A Falcon than to be

a Leg Pulling Crab.

To Know More: Infoline – 7781900870
Mail Us At-
flairsandglairs@gmail.com / info@flairsandglairs.in
Or Visit is at
www.flairsandglairs.com / www.flairsandglairs.in
Social Handles- @flairsandglairs @teekhezasbaaat